DUDE!

WORD BY
AARON REYNOLDS

PICTURES BY
DAN SANTAT

A NEAL PORTER BOOK
ROARING BROOK PRESS
NEW YORK

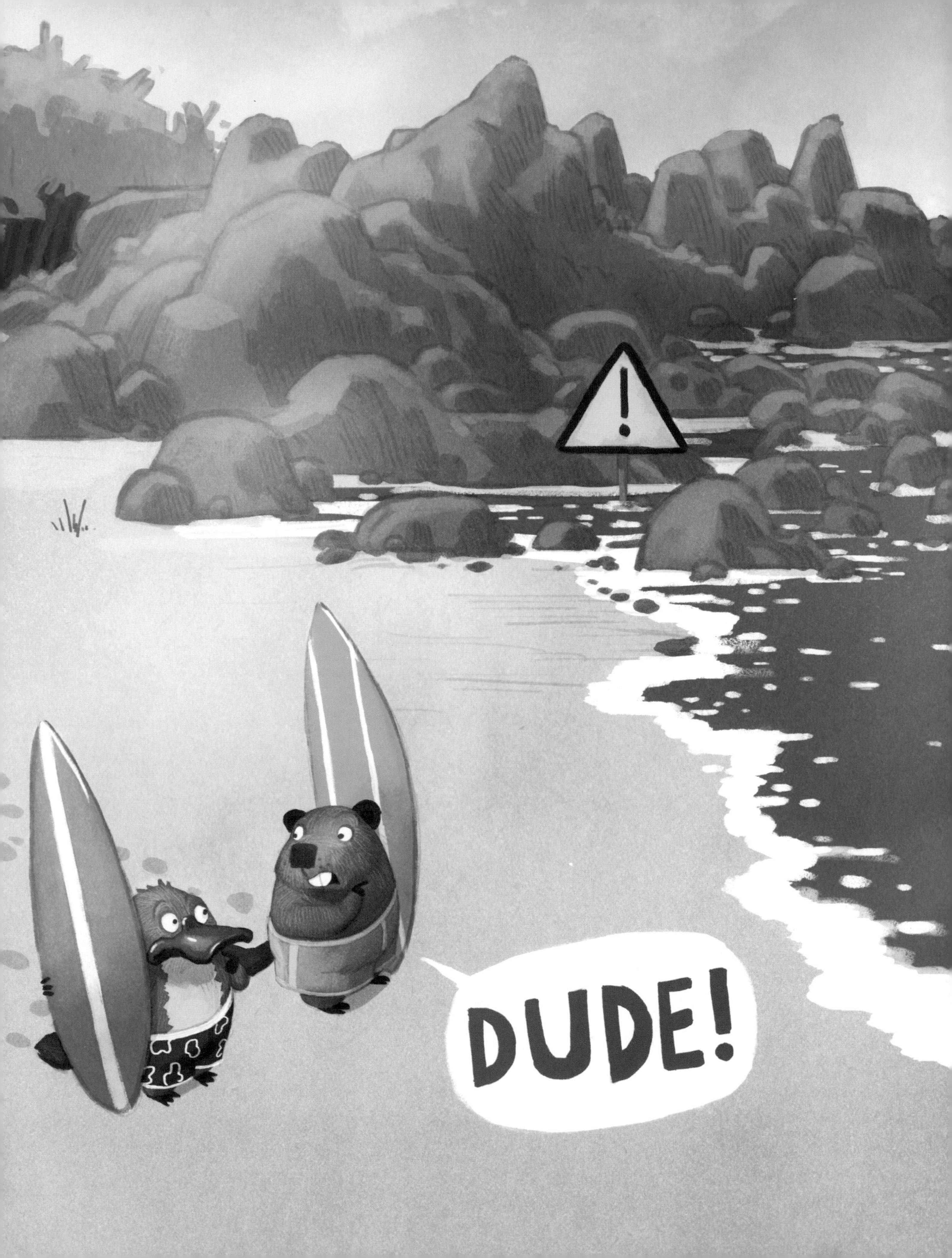
DUDE!

Dude!

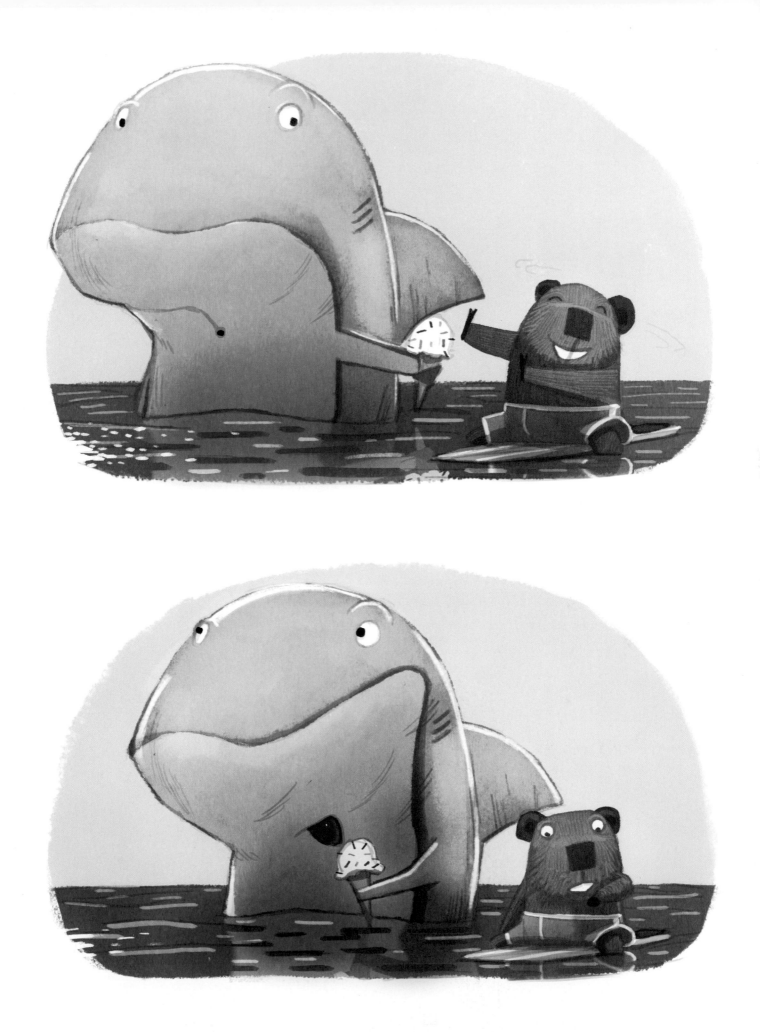

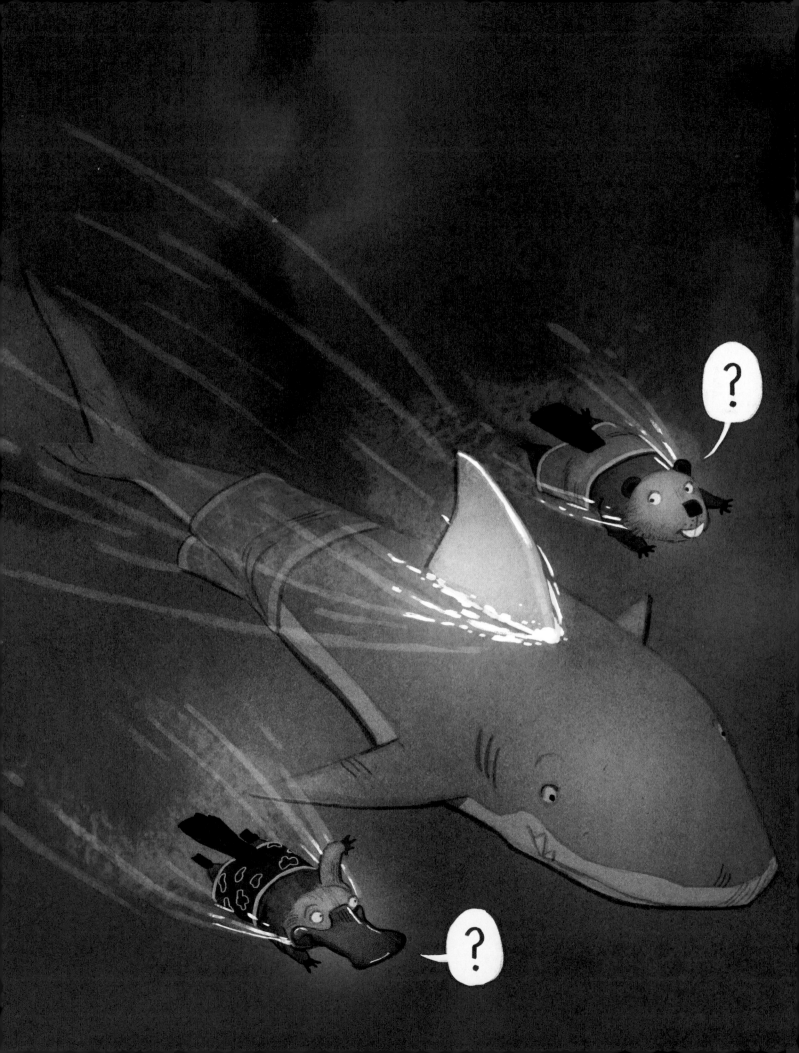

Text copyright © 2018 by Aaron Reynolds
Illustrations copyright © 2018 by Dan Santat
A Neal Porter Book
Published by Roaring Brook Press
Roaring Brook Press is a division of Holtzbrinck Publishing Holdings Limited Partnership
175 Fifth Avenue, New York, NY 10010
mackids.com

Library of Congress Control Number: 2017944502

Hardcover ISBN: 978-1-62672-603-1
Kohl's edition ISBN: 978-1-250-23988-4

KOHL'S
Style: 1250239885
Factory Number 123386
5/19–7/19

This special edition was printed for Kohl's Department Stores Inc. (for distribution on behalf of
Kohl's Cares, LLC, its wholly owned subsidiary) by Roaring Brook Press.

Our books may be purchased in bulk for promotional, educational, or business use.
Please contact your local bookseller or the Macmillan Corporate and Premium Sales Department
at (800) 221-7945 ext. 5442 or by e-mail at MacmillanSpecialMarkets@macmillan.com.

First edition 2018
Kohl's edition, 2019
Book design by Andrew Arnold
Printed in China by RR Donnelley Asia Printing Solutions Ltd., Dongguan City, Guangdong Province

1 3 5 7 9 10 8 6 4 2